George Macdonald Mair

The bride of Bar-Cocab

A tale in verse

George Macdonald Mair

The bride of Bar-Cocab
A tale in verse

ISBN/EAN: 9783337174682

Printed in Europe, USA, Canada, Australia, Japan

Cover: Foto ©Andreas Hilbeck / pixelio.de

More available books at **www.hansebooks.com**

THE

BRIDE OF BAR-COCAB.

A TALE IN VERSE,

BY

GEORGE MACDONALD MAIR.

———

NEW YORK :

C. WESLEY JONES.

218 FULTON STREET,

1882.

"IF I HAVE DONE WELL, AND AS IS FITTING THE STORY, IT IS THAT WHICH I DESIRED, BUT IF SLENDERLY AND MEANLY, IT IS THAT WHICH I COULD ATTAIN UNTO."

II MACCABEES, XV: 38.

NOTE.

Coziba, a Jewish rebel, in the reign of the Roman Emperor Hadrian, having assumed the title of Bar-Cocab—the son of a star—in allusion to Balaam's prophecy (Num. xxiv: 17.) and proclaimed himself Messiah, over 200,000 Jews rallied around his standard. This immense host was utterly routed at Bitthera. a fortified city a few leagues from Jerusalem, by the Roman Governor of Judea ; Coziba himself being slain. The fiction that his *fiancée* on the evening preceding the battle revealed to him her conversion to Christianity and urged him to retire from the contest, as related in the poem. and the whole of the second canto are, of course. deviations from historical verity.

THE BRIDE OF BAR-COCAB.

CANTO THE FIRST.

I.

'Mid groves of figs and olive wood,
　　O'ershadowed by the sacred fanes
　　Of Salem on the higher plains,
The city of Bitthera stood ;
That fortress where, of old, along
Those hills once refluent with song,
The mightiest army took its stand
That Israel could to arms command
Since Titus' victory laid the shrine

In ashes, fondly deemed divine.
Far off, and semi-circling high,
The peaks of Moab bound the eye,
And form, since further sight is ceased,
The blue horizon of the east,
And, nearer, in the shadow seen,
The arid desert drifts between,
And, westward, when the eye has passed
Of the uneven hills, the last,
The land in one descending plain
Slopes gently to that tideless main
That softly laps or wildly raves
Its impotent and harmless waves.

II.

Bitthera—who of all that tread
That spot, its tale have rightly read?
Or pause to pay the homage there
Such hallowed scenes should ever share?
For there, though crushed by weary years
Of vassal life and exile tears,

The slumbering heroism woke,
Of souls that chafed beneath the yoke,
While faltering Freedom, loth to flee
The clime of her nativity,
Still tarried with the hearts of flame
That to her final rally came:
There, on that very field arrayed
The last, fond, vain attempt was made.
Yet few—ah none— e'er stop to trace
The mournful history of the place,
Or grant the tribute of a tear
To memories Freedom should revere;
For such the vandalism of Time,
And famine's dearth and despot's crime,
That not a vestige now is there
To point their courage or despair,
And even tradition lingers not
To sanctify th' neglected spot,
Or aid him whose unworthy verse
Would seek the story to rehearse.

III.

The eve falls soon, but lingering still,
Day trails in beauty o'er the hill,
As to dispel with lovelier light
The gathering darkness of the night.
The breeze is sprung and wafts along
    The odorous breath of wild-grown flowers,
The echoes of the bird's last song,
    Still floating through the woody bowers,
The dew is fallen on bud and leaf
That seem the fairer in their grief;
Above, the mellow moon is bright,
Without a cloud to veil her light,
And the hushed stars upon the coast
Of heaven array their twinkling host
And shine that softness o'er the hour,
Oh! who has loved nor felt its power!

IV.

Within a bower by sheltering trees
    Protected from Intrusion's gaze,

Mine eye a sudden vision sees,
Obscure at first, but, by degrees,
  In bold relief the scene I trace :
  A man of sad, upbraiding face,
  And, by his side, a form of grace,
  The Dryad of this lonely place.
Far, far, they've left behind, I ween,
Their native and familiar scene
Whate'er their errand is, and here
Are safe from any listening ear.
Thus much I reason from the sweat
With which the chargers' flanks is wet,
That, tethered near for instant aid,
Crop lazily the grassy glade,
Whose strong, lithe limbs in time of need,
Might well be deemed a thing of speed.

V.

An open helmet lies hard by
  The mound on which they sit, as though
He felt it weigh oppressively

And had removed it from his brow.
A coat of mail enwraps his breast,
And greaves around his legs are laced.
Beside his helmet, too, are laid
A Spanish sword of finest blade,
And, ready for his instant grasp,
The pilum, such as Romans clasp,
But all appear, in sooth, alien
At such a time, in such a scene.

VI.

But not alone his garb betrays
A want of harmony with the place,
I see it in his gloomy face ;
For o'er that brow is darkening there
The shadow of a crushing care,
That seems a shade less than despair.
All feelings that the heart can know—
Regret, defeated hope, and woe,
The passion-chaos of the breast,
I trace upon his face impressed ;

Yet, conquering all, and chastening down
Each hasty word and rising frown,
I note that gentleness of love,
That sorrow's tempest could not move,
That bade the will of self be spurned,
And ceased t' upbraid even while it mourned.

VII.

And she, whose story he had heard
And quivered at each blighting word,
That to his boding heart had seemed
The knell of all he hoped or dreamed,
She turns her gaze on him, her eye
Filled with the tear of sympathy,
As one whose heart had felt constrained
To tell the secret it contained,
Yet mourned each word it had to speak—
But oh! that dewy eye and cheek,
Seemed to have added loveliness,
If such could be, in her distress;
And those fair lips, that arching brow,

Had ne'er so tempting been as now,
When sorrowing for another's woe.
How tame then must my verse express
The increase of that loveliness,
Which was a thing far too divine
For human language to define,
The outward profile it might give,
But not the soul that made it live,
And lit the beauty of that face
With something more than earthly grace:
A halo from the blessed place!

VIII.

"Oh Ruth! of all my foes," he said,
"From thee I have the most to dread,
Thy frown can do my heart more harm
   Than Roman power, or Roman guile,
For victory loses half its charm
   If unrewarded by thy smile.
Oh! oft I've scorned the coward soul
Whose valor owned a maid's control,

And scoffed the courage such supplies
In ruby lips or sparkling eyes,
But Love has wrought his own revenge
And seared a heart he shall not change.
Too true, they say, who call the love
  Of woman but a fickle thing—
A fancy which a glance can move,
  And just as quickly put to wing."

IX.

"Nay, but indeed thou art unjust,"
She answered to his closing thrust,
"Did I not love thee more than life
I would not risk mine in such strife,
Nor leave my family and my home,
Such uncongenial scenes to roam,
Nor brave it, since arise it must,
The scandal, too, like thee, unjust.
And if, in sooth, my faith is changed,
My heart from thee is not estranged.
Oh! little dost thou reck the pain,

Unrested heart and weary brain,
The long, long days of doubts and fears,
The nights that seemed prolonged to years,
Before my heart and mind and will,
Half won and half rebellious still,
Made full surrender to the creed
That wakes thy bitterest hate and deed.
But whose the fault? if fault there be
It rests with thee, Bar-Cocab, thee.
The Christian captive was thy friend,
To whom thou bad'st me to extend
Such courtesy as he might claim
That would not compromise my name:
I gave such care, the white-haired man
Whose years were running o'er their span,
Beguiled the weary hours of death
With histories of his life and faith.
I saw in death his eyelids close
As fearless as a babe's repose,
And yet a captive and with foes!

He was in life and death a saint
Who made no murmur nor complaint,
In all those weary months of grief,
Nor sighed for freedom nor relief.
What marvel that the faith whose power
Sustained him through each lonely hour,
Found me unable thus to cope,
With no such faith and no such hope,
And conquered when my heart found peace
By resting on that Cross and grace.
Oh! darling, scoffer as thou art,
Oh! let that Cross subdue thy heart.
For dark, indeed, the end I see
Of this wild life will prove to thee,
And darker still, perchance, to me!"

X.

"I? God of Abraham forbid!
That were worse sin than Israel did,
When in the wilderness they prayed
Unto the idol Aaron made.

It were strange humor in my spleen
To bow before the Nazarene,
Who have made many of his faith
To join him in his felon's death.
Would such had been the bishop's fate!
Nor had I been compassionate,
Save that my sire once owed his life
To his strong arm in battled strife,
In earlier years upon the field,
When both a patriot's sword did wield
Against the foe I fight (that deed
Was ere he had abjured his creed.)
And well my kindness he repaid,
To proselyte a guileless maid,
But say no more—a faithless name,
The taunt of an apostate's shame
Shall never darken my fair fame.
Nor time, however dark my deed,
E'er prove me recreant to my creed!

XI.

"Nay, Israel's God once more shall bless
With choicest gifts His chosen race.
Dost think He can forswear His oath
As lightly as a maid her troth?
Or deem that Israel ne'er shall taste
The future that her seers forecast?
Nay, Israel's sins and cowardice
Have barred us from the Paradise
Our God reserves for him whose faith
   Can trust His promises, nor cower
Beneath a mortal tyrant's wrath
   While resting on Almighty power.
As Joshua dared and Gideon,
So may I be their worthy son!
But come, whatever fate be mine
   The die is cast—I shall not shrink,
I have but one life to resign,
   And should my trampled country sink
To deeper subjugation, I

Would rather in her service die,
Than live to linger out my days
The slave the heathen tyrant sways.—
Come, let us to the tent return
    And hide thy secret in thy breast,
    Lest even I could not arrest
The vengence I alone should mourn."

XII.

She rose and stood irresolute;
    Then flung herself upon his breast,
And hung her head a moment mute,
    By love and sorrow both possessed—
"Say, dearest—oh! too dear thou art!
Come, let me read thine inmost heart.
Because my childhood's faith is changed,
Say, is thy love from me estranged?
I charge thee, let thy words be sooth,
Oh dost thou love me still in truth?
If not, oh send me from thee now,
Yet not in words the change avow;

I could not bear to hear those lips
Pronounce affection's harsh eclipse ;
Nor yet could bear with thee to stay,
And know that love had died away ;
But rather let me go alone,
Nor hear thy heart's dread, altered tone.
There is a solitary place
For those who know the heavenly grace,
Where woman may renounce for e'er
The outside world and all its care,
And spend her life in fasts and prayer.
The God who gave His Son for me,
Will guide my footsteps as I flee.
Such would I seek and there forget,
    Perchance, my unrequited love.
Oh ! if thou dost not love me yet
    Let my last wish thy bosom move."

XIII.

He rained upon her upturned lips
    Fierce kisses, passionate and fast—

"Not love thee, sweet? the insect sips
  From many flowers a flippant taste;
So may the dainty soldier change
His love from pique or for revenge;
Not I, the love I did avow
Is changeless, naught could change it now.
Not even betrayed, yet constant still,
My heart could not desire thee ill.
And yet this very constancy
But gives a deeper pang to me.
For I had dreamed thee by my side
My counsellor as well as bride,
The star of hope that led me on
  From victory to victory,
Whose smile was worth a battle won,
  And bade the fears of sorrow flee.
And heard in my prophetic ear
The tidings of my triumph near,
And felt anticipation bless
My spirit with assured success,

Until the plastic present seemed
Almost the future that I dreamed.
Once more had Israel in that hour
Regained her ancient, regal power,
Once more my trampled country bloomed,
My race their glorious march resumed,
And I their king and thou my queen,
Had reaped the blessings of the scene,
The benedictions freely given
To instruments thus blessed of heaven,
Who make a people's slavery cease,
And win them liberty and peace,
And been unto all future days
The patriot's type, the poet's praise."

XIV.

"Bar-Cocab, oh! I weep to know
How sure such dreams must wake in woe.
How fair soe'er the prospects seem,
They're even vainer than a dream.
Let reason teach how weak indeed

Such paltry force is to succeed,
The merest fraction at the most,
To what the Roman power can boast,
In arms and hardihood and skill
The difference more unequal still.
Oh, vain the hope of aught to be
But dire disaster unto thee!
And to what haven canst thou flee?
Since all the world has no retreat,
But suppliant kneels at Caesar's feet;
More hopeless still, for who would rue
The sorrows of an outcast Jew?
Or dare offend the serfs of Rome,
By offering him a rest or home.
Nor death, that crowns a soldier's fame,
To thee, would only seal thy shame,
Since whate'er aspirations high
Inspire thy soul to win or die,
The world has placed thee by her ban
A brigand chief—an outlawed man,

Whose bravery is a desperate deed,
Whose sole ambition—lust of greed,
And ignorant of thy better will
The stigma would o'ershade thee still.
Oh yield, if reason will not move,
Oh yield a captive unto love."

XV.

"My men are outlaws, it is true,
But yet they only seek their due.
Driven in exile from their land,
    And spurned alike in Greece or Rome,
They know on earth no friendly hand,
    They see no hope, they have no home.
The soil the tyrant lends to-day
To-morrow's greed may rend away,
And even life—the tyrant's hate
Regards no rights inviolate,
A Jew weighed in a Roman scale
Is lower than the slave of sale,
The ready prey at any hour

Of him whose hand possesses power.
What can they do then save to turn
Upon the ruthless foes that spurn,
And grasp by the same methods, life,
And wealth, and power, by Ishmael strife!
And what to me is life and fame
The while my country lies in shame?
Oh! glance it over from this height,
Beneath the moon's refulgent light,
And feel the worship of the sight!
Behold our sacred city's fanes
That ne'er a worshipper contains ;
Behold those glorious fields and hills,
Which now a foreign despot tills,
And tell me if one might not bleed
With rapture for to see them freed
From his accursed power—yea, die
With triumph in his closing eye!
My spirit thrills as here I stand
　　And scan those holy haunts where once

Men heard from heaven divine response,
My disinherited fatherland!
Which to describe is poetry,
   And even now seems floating there
   A spirit in the viewless air
That bids thy people yet be free.

XVI.

"Wild Paradise! even in neglect,
   Thy weeds of widowhood are fair,
Although no loving hand has decked
   For weary years thy disrepair.
Still partial Nature strives to veil
The wrecks of Time and ruin's trail,
Profusely still her gifts are strown
   In this one spot of sacred soil,
That elsewhere bless no single zone,
   But ask a world-wide clime and toil.
The spicy winds from orient shores
Purloin for thee their richest stores,
And all that greets the traveler's quest

In dewy south or cooler west,
Are lavished on thy valleys fair
And tempt the wanderer lingering there ;
While even the Alpine flower buds blow
Upon thy mountain crests of snow,
Whate'er the whole wide world can show—
All—tributary here combine
To make this miniature world of thine.
While ever loving heaven supplies
Her brighest stars and bluest skies,
And o'er the pleasant landscape throws
An air of peace and calm repose.

XVII.

"But these are all that cannot die ;
  All else of glory and of grace
  Have faded and have left no trace,
Like rainbows in a summer sky.
Of art or beauty of thine own
There is no vestige, not a stone
Remains where once thy temple stood

To sanctify the solitude.
The voices of thy seers are hushed,
The spirit of thy sons is crushed :
No more against Oppression's rod
They rise to wreak the wrath of God ;
Save when some outlaw on the hill
Strikes one frail blow for vengeance still.
The song of mirth is heard no more,
Nor festal dance along thy shore,
Save when the harp that was divine
Is struck by other hands than thine ;
For thine have been the deadliest foes
That e'er a people's history shows,
War, famine, pestilence, and all
That darkens nations with a pall,
Have been thy heritage of ill,
My country, and afflict thee still.

XVIII.

"Ah me, when Memory loses sway,
Then bid me turn from Vengeance' way.

When I forget the deadly wrongs
That now my recollection throngs,
The years of shame, the dark disgrace,
That conquers, then corrupts, a race.
When I can fawn and praise the Power
That brought the sorrows of this hour,
If Justice suffers me to live,
Then come and pray me to forgive.
But may the blackest curses rest
Upon the recreant, coward breast,
That for a moment's pause would turn
To cease to make th' oppressor mourn,
Or opportunity forsake
Its hatred in his blood to slake !
May heaven turn from his prayer to save !
May earth deny the wretch a grave !
And all the powers of hell arise
To lengthen out his agonies,
Till even the fiends shrink in dismay,
From one far more accursed than they !"

XIX.

He helped her mount, then grasped his blade
  And ponderous pilum from the ground,
  Leaped on his steed with one light bound,
And home they galloped through the glade.
They rode in silence; bright above
The moon its radiant pathway clove,
Its white beams softly round them thrown
On tree and vine, unheeded shone.
Bright as the stars above the bloom
Of snowy blossoms wept perfume.
The phlox in pinky beauty set,
The asphodel and mignonette,
The wild-rose with its blushing flowers,
Unnoticed gemmed the grassy bowers.
Yet 'mid the stillness of the scene,
They felt their hearts grow more serene.
His disappointment and distress
Lost half its venomed bitterness,
And she unwinged her hopes to soar

To brighter visions than before,
And viewed him, snatched from ban and death
A happy convert to her faith.
Oh! who e'er felt his spirit shrink
From cares 'neath which he must not sink,
And let the midnight breezes blow
O'er waving hair and throbbing brow,
Nor felt his burdens grow more light
Beneath the cooling touch of Night?
Sweet hour! whose stillness seems a prayer
Though voiceless, o'er the brow of Care!

XX.

Yet as he rode against his will
Some sad reflections pressed him still,
With all the heaviness and force
Of him who feels a recent loss.
For the companion at his side
Had been a help-meet, loved and tried.
Since both had conned the sacred page
Together from an early age,

And felt their hearts harmonious burn,
To see those glorious times return.
In all his schemes her interest lent
To him a dear encouragement,
Though oft they woke in her more zeal,
Than his less sanguine breast could feel.
But all this sympathy to-night
Died in the altered proselyte,
Whose eyes beheld with different sight,
And now believed those hopes to be
To God presumptuous enmity.
And, though so flippantly dismissed
The words, that Ruth had scarcely wist
They gained a moment's thought—his heart
Had felt them like a venomed dart.
They surged it now with angry shame
When he recalled his blighted name,
Who far and near had thus been banned
The leader of a wild command,
And she alone had understood

The thought of his heroic mood;
For even his men were slow to learn
The higher hopes she could discern,
Nor dreamed a higher aim was his
   Than greed of wealth and lust of power,
Nor knew that life possessed no bliss
   While Israel was the Roman's dower,
Nor e'er had pierced his deeper mind
To see they were by him designed
To be the nucleus of strength
To raze the Cæsar's throne at length :
Each member of the band a Jew
To memory and to vengeance true,
Selected with consummate skill
A tool to serve their leader's will,
Until at last his plans matured,
A powerful host his call secured ;
The proud and world-wide empire through,
A new ambition seized the Jew,
The artisan forsook his trade

The trembling merchant grasped a blade,
And in Bar-Cocab hoped to see
A second, greater Maccabee,
And to his standard lent such aid
That careless Cæsar felt dismayed.

XXI.

The offspring of a priestly sire—
   His grandsire had beheld the doom
   Of Israel by the power of Rome,
Had seen her temple wreathed in fire,
Had seen her liberties expire,
   And in her service found a tomb.
From whence Bar-Cocab's soul had caught
The animus of deeds thus wrought,
Which in his more susceptive years
His mother taught his greedy ears,
By whom he had been dedicate
To bear to Rome unchanging hate,
Repledged upon her bed of death,
And well he kept that awful faith :

By many a village given to flame,
And many a deed of blood and shame,
And many a tax·and treasure sent
The coffers of the government,
Spoiled by his lawless horde, attest
That vengeance slept not in his breast.

XXII.

Yet lives of shame and deeds of blood,
Were not to him congenial mood,
Nor sought because he found delight
In slaughter, and a bliss in fight.
Phenomenal men in epoch times
Commit what were in others, crimes:
He deemed the end he had in view,
Absolved the means he did pursue
As being to him, the instrument
To carry out his high intent.
This warped his judgment till t' obtain
Success, he spared no cost nor pain,
And worse, it chilled his yielding heart,

When Mercy bade compassion start,
Till, as the Gorgon looked upon
The form that glance transformed to stone,
He ceased to mourn the hearts that bled,
Or shudder at the carnage red,
However dark the deed of blight
Supporting the imagined right.
Still, even his worst extreme was less
Than methods of the foe's success,
And he could palliate his hate
By pointing to his country's state,
While Rome upon her seven hills
For selfish luxury wrought her ills.

XXIII.

His years fell short of middle age
And yet his mind was formed as sage,
Such years, though few indeed their span,
Transform even youthhood into man.
Beset with dangers and with foes,
The heart's deep longings, fears and woes,

The mind's intensest tension stretched
To work the plan its high hope sketched,
These all were his, and marked his face
With those stern lines such lifetimes trace.
His laugh was far more grave than gay,
His hair was prematurely gray,
And yet withal no daintier face
Had ever won a maiden's praise,
Nor sweeter voice, nor milder art,
E'er overcome an obdurate heart,
Or supplicated Beauty's shrine,
Than masked that outlaw's bold design.

XXIV.

'Twas yet three hours ere Morn should rise
And veil the stars in eastern skies
When lo! they saw beneath their light
A splendid though expected sight.

XXV.

Far as the mounted eye could reach,
  Encamped along the broad champaign

Like sands upon the river beach,
  A tented army stretched of men.
Wide circling all, an earthen mound
Full ten feet high, formed ample bound
On whose unbroken height arrayed,
Was built a dangerous palisade,
Protected on the outer side
By ditches ten feet deep and wide.
Distinguished by its greater height
The general's quarters met the sight,
Within the central space and round
The others had their proper bound.
The footman sleeping by his spear,
The horseman and his charger near,
And martial engines further rear,
Where sleepless vigil did secure
The baggage and the furniture,
All drawn in as exact array
As Cæsar's legions might display.

XXVI.

In answer to some secret sign,
The sentinel brought them in the line.
Where willing hands were waiting there
To render every needed care.
The lady sought her private tent,
The chief to his, his pathway bent,
And of his armor there undressed,
Sought fruitlessly an hour of rest,
While she with less unquiet mind,
Soon found the sleep he failed to find.

XXVII.

At last upon his eyelids pressed
The semblance of refreshing rest,
When there arose a shout so loud,
That thunder from the breaking cloud
Reverberating overhead,
Would seem to peal less deep and dread.
And on the eastern palisade,
A yawning breach he saw, dismayed.

So suddenly the crumbling clay
Fell through or in the ditches lay,
It seemed more like the earthquake's shock,
Than battering-ram or darted rock,
And such his semi-conscious thought
Had deemed the breach and the report
Had not his eyes seen through it poured
The masses of the Roman horde,
And heard the trumpets sound alarms,
And sentries cry "to arms! to arms!"

XXVIII.

Attached to Bar-Cocab's command
There was a straggling motley band,
Untrained in arms. Of some the aim
Was plunder—some had fled from shame,
Both men and women—young and fair—
And even old Age crouched trembling there,
Who fled to find a kinder life
Although 'mid Battle's awful strife,
Than bear their lords' imperious mood.

Or live in soulless servitude ;
These skirted the great host and fell
At the first onslaught in the dell.
As when some landslide crunches down
The mountain side upon the town,
Or when in northern seas the ice
Towers high like craggy precipice,
And crushes into instant death
The hapless ship that steers beneath,
So, helplessly, they meet the blow
And fall before the ruthless foe,
And, maddened in their wild affright,
Like frightened game confuse their sight,
And trample down a greater host
Than even the enemy's sword can boast—
Men, women, children madly mixed,
Trampled to death, by spears transfixed.
How savage was the carnage there
When selfishness urged on despair.
And neither age nor youth could stay,

Nor beauty awe the lust to slay.

XXIX.

Stunned for the moment and amazed,
Bar-Cocab at the conflict gazed,
As still in doubt but all might be,
His sleep's disordered reverie.
Till, cleaving through his open tent,
A pilum fell with force unspent
And passing by, so near him pressed
It almost grazed his unmailed breast.
Admonished thus, he quickly dressed
In armor, now too long delayed,
And firmly grasped his Spanish blade,
    And caught his pilum in his hand,
And to the front his progress made,
    To win or perish with his band.
Once there, his pilum had such aim
As two to kill, a third to maim;
And he such greeting gave his foes,
That few dared stand before the blows.

XXX.

His advent seemed to give new life
Unto his followers in the strife,
Who rush impetuously along
Against the overwhelming throng,
And many a Roman soldier dies
As fast and fierce the pilum flies:
And as from numbers they withstand,
The combat changes hand to hand ;
The broadswords in the sunlight flash,
The gore spurts red from many a gash.
While some with the barbarian's mace,
On either side maintain their place,
Until the field is red with blood,
And pools of the ensanguined flood
Congeal, where, on the fetid plain
The bodies lie of maimed and slain.

XXXI.

The cavalry, whose greater host   .
The martial power of Rome could boast,

Became, so fierce was the onslaught,
Detached from where the others fought,
And met upon the southern field—
 With deadly power the Romans threw
 Their solid phalanx on the Jew,
Who pledged to rather die than yield,
With awful shock against them wheeled,
 And stood their ground, tho' many a horse
Dashed from their ranks whose rider reeled
 And fell to earth a mangled corse.
Again the deadly charge—again
The wild repulse of desperate men,
In bloodier combat than before,
Themselves, their chargers, smeared with gore
And maddened ranks thinned more and more!
And yet again the sickening thud
Of the opposing foes—the blood
That from the men and horses flood!
Then the irregular sallies, where
The Jews surrendered to despair,

Whose only hope was in the strife,
To dearly sacrifice each life,
And glut defeat with foeman's blood,
Till after the last rally stood,
Of all Bar-Cocab's men but one—
Brave, bloody, reckless and alone.

XXXII.

The Roman horsemen ceased their strife,
And offered to parole his life ;
Admiring, envying, him possessed
The stoic valor of his breast.
He scoffed the life they would have freed
And dashed the rowels in his steed,
And ere they saw his purpose dread,
His sword had cleft the leader's head,
Another and another dies
Before they wake from their surprise ;
And hesitating then to strike,
Another Roman meets the like,
So rash, so dread, the soul can dare

In the wild fury of despair;
But that last stroke hath cost him dear,
He ne'er shall strike another here !

XXXIII.

In many quarters of the field,
   Bar-Cocab's mounted form was seen ;
   His life, a charmèd life had been
That day, for many a form had reeled
In death, that by his side had rode ;
But scathless still, though hued with blood
He rode, inciting courage where
The arm, at times, slacked in despair ;
Until he reached the sheltered tent
Wherein his lady-love was pent.
He paused a moment to assure
His heart she was within secure,
When lo ! as if with wings endued,
   She past him quickly, wildly, ran
   So swift, she did not see him then,
And by two Romans fast pursued.

Bar-Cocab followed, gasping sunk
The first, a headless, quivering trunk,
When he himself beneath a blow
Struck by the second, tottered low,
Who waiting not to ascertain
If Bar-Cocab were stunned, or slain,
Pursued, with still more eager pace,
The maid whose beauty lured his chase.

XXXIV.

As her pursuer drew more near
Her heart and brain throbbed wild with fear,
Which winged her speed that to the eye
Her dainty feet appeared to fly ;
She scarcely noticed where, or why,
The road she took—'twas soaked with blood,
 And now and then her fleet foot slid,
 So slippery and unsafe it did
Make all beneath its clotted flood ;
But this she had not time to think,
Nor of the eyes that seemed to blink

Upon her from the field of death,
As on she flew with bated breath.
At times she passed two living foes
Whose arms in deadly conflict close,
Or, now and then, a group who turn
To cheer her as her swift feet spurn
The ground, or blush for very shame
As on her vile pursuer came ;
But none essayed to aid her too,
For was she not by race a Jew ?

XXXV.

How long she fled she could not tell :
The moments to her frenzied fears
Prolonged themselves to months and years,
The distance stretched to many a league
Of footsore hardship and fatigue,
Until the landscape seemed to swim
Then fade in darkness—every limb
Unto its utmost tension taxed,
Quick as an eye could wink, relaxed

Its faithless strength and seemed to be
  Palsied in her extremity;
With a despairing shriek she fell,
His ruffian hand felt on her laid,
His breath upon her hot cheek played,
She dared not look into his face—
And yet—who spoke those words of grace?
Was it a dream? or did her ear
In truth those accents really hear?
Sweet words, that bade her fear no more,
But rest protected by his power,
That on her ears far sweeter fell
Than welcome after long farewell,
Or to the exile far away
The voice that sings his native lay,
Or gracious Beauty's longed for 'yes'
To Love's impatient eagerness.

XXXVI.

It was no dream, for bending o'er,
  With courteous solicitude,

She saw a face whose features wore
  The impress of a noble mood ;
Whose words assured her of a friend,
And brought her terrors to an end ;
And near him, stood the ruffian there
Whose evil spirit mourned to spare,
· Even while he sullenly obeyed
The order that his general made,
And left them at his stern command
Once more on bloody fields to stand.

XXXVII.

"I am the Roman Governor," said
Her new-found friend ; "be not dismayed ;
Nor harm nor fear shall follow thee,
As mine own sister thou shalt be.
But thou art tired—I will provide
An escort for thee, and a guide
To bring thee to my house and there
Thou wilt receive the tender care,
And the repose thou need'st to share."

And ere she could reply, he gave
The order to his waiting slave,
Who finding an escort and horse,
   By sheltered pathways guided them,
Until they reached, in rapid course,
   The mansion in Jerusalem.
And left th' exhausted maiden there,
To find repose and loving care;
While they returned unto the field,
In hopes it might some booty yield.

XXXVIII.

The strife was o'er—that noonday sun
That saw the hard fought battle won,
His vivid beams of yellow light
Cast on a saddening, sickening sight.
Of thousands that awoke that morn
With hopes to see another dawn,
Scarce hundreds marked the noon-day glare
That lit the field of slaughter there,
And they were prisoners, save a few

Who finally for safety flew,
Yet both, perchance, had better died
In battle by their comrades' side.

XXXIX.

Bar-Cocab whom the Governor sought
Was not among the prisoners brought,
Nor to his inquiry could relate
A soldier what had been his fate,
Until the latest straggler came
And gained a transitory fame
　　By tidings that were not gainsaid.
"I struck him down upon the field,
Then sought what other scenes might yield.
　　Supposing I had struck him dead.
Returning later in the day
To where I left his body lay,
　　I found that he had risen and fled ;
What further fate befell his lot,
Escaped or fallen—I know it not."

XL.

The Governor placed upon his head
A large reward—alive or dead;
If dead 'twere worth the price to know
The future free from that dread foe,
If living, fortunate the hour
That paid to hold him in his power :
But still suspense the less annoyed,
Since all his army was destroyed,
So thought he, as he turned his rein
To reach Jerusalem again ;
His men to follow when they'd paid
Their pious duty to the dead.

XLI.

'Twas noon—'tis night, who wanders there,
   At this lone hour among the dead,
   When even the spoiler flees with dread,
With gory face and clotted hair !
   Ah me! how changed! and yet I trace
   Bar-Cocab's features in his face,

Unarmed he stands with forehead bare ;
Then leaves the field with hurried tread,
   But pauses on the lonely hill,
   Where he can see Jerusalem still,
Or turning, view the sacred dead.
Hark ! borne along the summer air
His farewell message of despair.

XLII.

"Oh Israel ! captive and forlorn,
Alas ! that I have lived to mourn !
Of thousands of thy people strown
In death, why was I spared alone,
To see the tyrant's swelling host,
And hear his loud triumphant boast ?
And watch the midnight of disgrace
Without a star, gloom o'er my race ?
Oh Death ! why hast thou stricken low
   Young hearts enamored still of life,
While I who wildly sought thy blow,
   Escaped unharmed from peril's strife !

XLIII.

"For I had fondly hoped to be
The promise of thy prophecy.
To place upon thy forehead fair
The diadem that thou should'st wear,
To hurl the despot from the throne,
Thy sovereigns ruled in ages gone,
And turn the weary tides of ill,
And show thy God was with thee still.
But I have brought thee deeper wrong
And stronger chains,—oh God! how long!

XLIV.

"Oh Thou! who clothed in living fire,
    Didst choose us for thine own—how long
Before the heathen feel thine ire,
    And meet thy vengeance for our wrong.
Behold on yonder bloody plain
The thousands of thy people slain,
And where a smiling city stood,
Behold a desolate solitude.

Oh! let Thine anger turn from us
To fall on those who spoil us thus,
And hasten the auspicious hour
That ushers in Messiah's power,
And ripens all the prophecy
I vainly dreamed fulfilled in me.

XLV.

"I see Him—worthier than I—
   I see His glory from afar,
When He shall bring salvation nigh,
   And chase the desolate clouds of war.
Yet shall He come to wear the crown
The ages keep for Him alone.
Once more these scenes with joy shall shine
That now in desolation pine,
And shadeless glory bloom instead,
And shine a halo 'round His head :
And thou, Jerusalem, shall be
   The sacred city of the earth,
When men from climes beyond the sea

Shall turn their reverent eyes to thee,
 And bow to thy superior worth;
From thee shall heavenly truth proceed,
By which the nations shall be freed,
When thou shalt bid their sorrows cease,
And breathe the benison of peace.
The glowing centuries shall endower
With all their wealth, thy gracious power,
All art, all knowledge, shall combine
To blend, like incense, at thy shrine.
And Justice, wed to Love, shall be
 The pillars of Messiah's throne;
And Kings shall bow the subject knee,
 And to his scepter yield their own.

XLVI.

"But thou, Oh Rome! mine enemy,
In my prophetic sight I see
That thou shalt cease to be the free;
 Thy glory is a blood-stained thing,
 Oh thou! who to thy yoke dost bring

The power and riches of the earth !
Thou shalt not always sit in mirth,
But sackcloth shall thy covering be.
Oh ! still uprear to heedless stars
    The conqueror's memorial arch,
Yoke captive sovereigns to his cars
    Of triumph, on the homeward march.
Still wrench from the defenceless East
The gems that glitter at the feast,
And cross the cold and dark blue wave
    That beats upon the distant shore,
    In very wantonness of power,
To make the naked savage slave.
But know—though thou canst smile to hear
    The captive clank his galling chain—
Eternal Justice hovers near
    To recompense thee for his pain.
The wail of subjugated climes
Shall yet prevail against thy crimes;
And, great and matchless as thou art

Thou yet shalt know a widowed heart,
And long and dark the years shall be
That number out thy infamy."

XLVII.

He ceased : one glance across the right
Where Salem's towers were bathed in light,
Then turning one long gaze to meet
The fatal field of his defeat—
And with an imprecation fierce
    He fled—my vision saw him till
    He reached the woods beyond the hill—
His further path it could not pierce.
Oh where could Hope a covert spread
Where he might safely rest his head !

END OF CANTO FIRST.

THE BRIDE OF BAR-COCAB.

CANTO THE SECOND.

I.

It is a festal scene to-night,
That through the Governor's lattice bright
Streams far and wide yon flashing light,
And shines within a gayer sight;
Where Beauty's undisputed power,
Alone controls th' ecstatic hour.
How fleet, to Music's lively sound,
The glittering feet the floor rebound,
While in the pauses of the dance,
Eyes smile to Love's imploring glance,

Or some to laughing circles throng
To list the voice of Beauty's song,
Or fence in dear but dread debate,
Where hearts are lost to some coquette,
Who, skilled in Cupid's fickle arts,
Prizes all but captured hearts.

II.

Ruth, whose fair, faultless form and face,
The Governor knew had added grace,
Unto the festival and court,
Importunate her presence sought,
But vainly, for her faith forbade
Such revels as the heathen had.
Yet through her open casement floats
The laughter and the music notes,
And through the darkness, glitters bright
The lamps' full radiance of light.
But both appeals passed lightly by,
Unheeded by her ear or eye,
For she recalls the eve she stood

Within the solitary wood,
  With him from whose firm-plighted faith,
Although since that dark morn of blood,
She heard no word of ill or good,
  She fears no frailty,—only death.

III.

A gentle knock upon the door,
Admission gave the Governor,
Who to her glanced surprise replied,
"Oh yes, I fled a coquette's side,
A pensive hour with thee to spend,
My lovely, but ascetic friend.
The festival seemed dull as care,
When thou—the fairest—wert not there.
Oh! had those eyes of thine there shone,
They had made every heart thine own!
But tell me why should'st thou refuse,
And let such charms die without use.
What harm to list to Music's sound,
Or in the harmless dance whirl round?

The flowers live through their summer day
As heaven designed, in mere display;
The birds make life a symphony,
And thou dost love their melody;
What evil then for thee, whose youth
Hath bloom and melody in sooth,
A festal night at times to spend,
Where social joy links friend to friend?"

IV.

"I have no logic," she replied,
"That would convert thee to my side;
But my own heart and life to-night
Bear witness that my course is right.
I, too, have vainly whirled along
To Music's notes among the throng,
And felt my cheek blush glad to hear
The flatteries told my giddy ear.
But while I felt the vain wish swell
I had no thought of heaven or hell,
No love for God, and sadder still,

If thought of, only scorned, His will.
But now since I have known His grace.
I find no joy in such a place ;
Where even of Pleasure's votaries
The heart unrested sighs for ease,
And midst the most tumultuous joy,
Unsated, feels the pleasure cloy,
Nor thee,—oh! surely life is more
Than the mere plaything of an hour,
But rather is a solemn trust,
For which to give accounting just.
The shadow of the Cross of Christ
    Is resting o'er the world beneath,
And that life-blood there sacrificed,
    Brings fuller life or dreader death.
It is the touchstone of the will
That tests its tide of good or ill,
And shows how runs the current broad,
    In unison or enmity,
With its orginal source in God :

How runs it, kindest friend, with thee?"

V.

"I have been from my very youth
A ceaseless searcher after truth,"
He said "I've turned to creeds effete,
To find some truth there lingering yet ;
I've tried them all, but only tried
To turn from each unsatisfied,
To find in each, though different, still
The same old superstitious ill,
To find in each misunderstood
Or silence as to the supreme good.
I've passed through all—from seeing God
In earth and sea and sky and flower,
And everything—himself and power,
Till now, in all my eye beheld,
I see no Deity unveiled,
Nor to my bended knees hath e'er
A God answered my fervent prayer.
But list—my life at any time

Hath been unsoiled by loathsome crime,
For even in my boyish blood
My heart obeyed and reverenced good ;
At thy command I will resign
This Governor's office which is mine,
And we will flee to some retreat
Where naught of sin our eyes shall meet ;
Once there, and thou my lawful bride,
Thy faith and prayer my soul shall guide.
To kneel and worship at thy side—
And if indeed the Cross reveals
The infinite heart that throbs and feels
For every pang of human woe,
And sees repentant sorrows flow,
If this indeed is infinite love,
I long, I thirst, such love to prove :
But thou, be thou the teacher there,
To teach my ignorance, join my prayer."

VI.

He paused—her vision on his face

Grew fixed as in its glance to trace
His inmost heart—his eyes of fire
Were filled with Love's devout desire,
Beyond the power of utterance there.
And her eyes dropped before the glare,
And filled with tears to answer, 'no.'
She strove to soften it—"I owe
    To thee what I can ne'er repay ;
Not life—I prize it not below—
    Had the wild ruffian sought to slay,
I had not fled nor feared the blow,
But more—what woman prizes most
And finds no substitute when lost—
Her virtue—through thy power and grace,
I 'scaped the soldier's vile embrace.
For this I thank thee, and my prayer
Shall make of thee a daily care,
My grateful praise, my heart's esteem,
While life holds out, or reason's beam
Is bright within me, shall to thee

Be given for thy clemency ;
And that is all I have—of love
One man alone my heart can move,
The love I plighted unto him,
Nor time can change nor distance dim.
And then besides I count my life
As much his as a wedded wife,
For with our nation, when a maid
Is once betrothed, 'tis ne'er betrayed,
Or to the recreant o'er her name,
The worst blight falls of sin and shame."

VII.

"Fair lady, (why art thou so fair ?)
    Bar-Cocab lives not—on the plain
    He was struck down with other slain.
'Tis the unreason of hope to bear
The thought that he has 'scaped from there,
Unless, indeed, he showed such care
For his own safety as to flee,
And think not, care not, what chanced thee :

In any case thou art set free.
Why nurse a love, then, in thy breast
That must forever be unblest?
And cast along thy future life,
Too young, too sweet, to fill with strife,
The shadow of a hopeless care,
Whose only courage is despair?"

VIII.

"Thou little reck'st what thou dost ask,"
She answered, "nor how false the mask
Which thou wouldst have me wear; for know
His love is all I prize below.
Nor would I change, even be he dead,
My affection for the spirit fled,
For any living lover here,
Nor could another be so dear. ·
For since my childhood's earliest bliss,
My life has been entwined with his,
The playmate of my youthful hours
In more propitious times and bowers,

And when years sped his breast was fired
To see his people's hopes expired,
I felt with him a mutual flame,
To turn the tide that flowed their shame.
I was his confidante—my ear
Drank greedily his hope and fear,
And eagerly we hoped, indeed,
And oft we talked of the high meed
That should reward the soul that freed.
And I with him oft shared the bliss,
Anticipative, that would be his,
And when my faith was changed, his heart
Was constant though pierced by a dart.
Yea, though I knew there was no pain
That man e'er felt in heart and brain,
More sharp than his when from my lips
He heard what seemed his hopes t' eclipse,
He loved me still, although his face
Worked, as his inmost thoughts did trace,
Upon it all the heart can know

Of baffled hope and sudden woe,
And even left me uncontrolled
To practice what my conscience told,
Although the creed my soul professed
Was most abhorrent to his breast.
Oh no! my heart where'er he be
Is wedded to his memory,
Nor can it know another love,
Or faithless to that memory prove."

IX.

"I ask no treachery," he said,
"Unto the memory of the dead.
Still let him have the prior part,
The first allegiance of thy heart,
I only ask a friend's esteem,
Which would not falsehood be to him :
No more than this from thee I'd claim,
Though pledged by ties of dearer name.
Since he is dead, oh! grant to me
The right to guide and succor thee :

As if the dead with his last word
Had willed it, that my suit be heard,
And had committed to me there
Thyself for my peculiar care.
Wait if thou wilt until thy grief
In time and distance finds relief,
To test my love and find it shown
Solicitous to win thine own;
But oh! deny me not to know
I'm dearer thee than all below.
Nay, give me no harsh answer now,
But ponder what I here avow.
I leave thee to thy solitude
To answer in a calmer mood,
And may my heart rejoice to find
Thy gracious will to me resigned."

X.

Days passed—again and oft renewed,
His ardent suit he still pursued,
With all the argument and art

That love assaults an obdurate heart. ·
But still, though madly he may cope
Her answer gave his heart no hope.
At last, as yielding to his fate
He seemed the less importunate,
A week had rolled away and then
Another ere he spoke again;
But oh ! how changed in that short time,
As by an age of grief and crime
His cheek, which had been fair with youth,
Was white and sunken, too, in sooth,
His brow, once smooth, was lined with pain,
And furrowed by each starting vein,
And his wild eye sepulchral shown
Bright, but its beam unearthly thrown ;
His hair unkempt, untrimmed his beard,
And every feature worn and weird,
And even his clothing disarranged---
Alas, indeed, how sadly changed !

XI.

"Forgive," she noticed as he spoke
How huskily the wild words broke,
"Forgive me if thou canst," he cried,
"The measures which despair may guide,
I can all hopes but thee resign,
I love thee, and thou shalt be mine,
If not persuasion, then must force,
In this last time be my resource."

XII.

With eyes that flashed and bosom heaving,
She turned upon him, scarce believing
The awful threat his words implied,
"I would not bend to thee," she cried
"Though thou didst to thy service bring
Captivity's most dreaded sting,
Shut the bright sun from these fond eyes,
Chain these frail limbs till each one dies.
And more than these, bring to thine aid,
The torture—I am not dismayed ;

I scorn thee and defy thee still,
And make no bending to thy will!"

XIII.

"Beware!" he answered "oh! beware,
Nor spurn me more than I can bear;
And think how near, ere 'tis too late,
Is unrequited love to hate."

XIV.

"Dost call this love? it only proves
Such heart as thine is, never loves.
Nay, slander not the word, nor prate
Of love that may be turned to hate.
Love is no courtier that displays
His loyalty on sunny days,
And changes when misfortune's hour
O'ercomes the reign of fickle power.
It has no ebb—it knows no change,
No jealousy and no revenge:
It has no self-will, but will blend
The way its deep affections tend.

As ever to its proper pole
The faithful needle owns control,
So love, though time or distance part,
Still pays the worship of the heart ;
That homage, which though unreturned,
Or scarcely owned or harshly spurned,
Becomes the temper of the soul,
And holds, unconsciously, control.
Aye, love can suffer and can wait,
But never fellowships with hate.
'Tis said that women's eyes soon learn
Love's latent presence to discern,
And such I feared was in thy breast ;
Yes, feared, since it must be unblessed,
Thy threats have proved thy care for me
Was less of love than vanity.
Brave man ! who stoops his glance to lour
Upon a captive in his power !
But know—I believe Bar-Cocab lives,
Thy fear a different answer gives,

And some day from thee will demand
The life thus thrown within thy hand.
Yet living or dead—hear thou my oath!
To thee I ne'er will plight a troth;
My vow recorded is on high,
Rather than wed thee I would die:
For heathen as thou art indeed,
In barbarous nature and in creed,
My faith forbids my life to be
Allied in marriage thus to thee.
Waste not thy words—thou canst not move
My heart—I scorn thy hate or love!"

XV.

"I thank thee for the thought—my power
Would safely shield in peril's hour
If love enlists its sympathy,
But oh—beware its enmity,
Thou dost reproach my pagan creed;
    Rash woman! dost forget thy faith
By Roman statutes is indeed

A crime adjudged deserving death!
Yet would my power protect thee still,
If thou art gracious to my will;
If not, then dread the worst extreme
That scoffed and maddened love may seem.
Thine is a woman's thought of love,
Whose symbol is the timid dove.
I cannot love and find it scoffed,
　And school my bursting heart and mind
　To meekly bear and be resigned;
My nature was not moulded soft.
My heart was made to love but once,
And love and find or force response.
If not, the scoffer shall not live
To mock my ruined hopes, and give
The preference to a rival's suit,
While I must worship and be mute.
Nay, now thou must decide thy fate.
Shall love shield love e'er 'tis too late,
Or dost thou scoff and brave my hate!

XVI.

"I, too, can love but once" she said,
"And having loved, my heart is dead
To all approach that could be made:
I do not fear thy power, but still
  I would not wish in aught to dare
  A desperate man's forlorn despair,
  Nor aught responsibility bear
For his wild deeds of crime and ill.
And yet the truth must still be said,
And thee I will not, cannot wed.
Yet---not because I fear the stake,
But let me plead for thine own sake:
Beware e'er thy despair's resource
Shall be a lifetime's vain remorse,
For oh! too plainly can I see
'Twill bring more ill to thee than me.
Such deeds so chill the guilty heart.
Repentance oft can find no part.
Then think how dread thy doom will be

Throughout a lost eternity."

XVII.

"'Tis idle thus to threaten woe
To one who bliss can never know ;
My love seems impotent to move
Thy bosom to responsive love;
Then take my hate, and with it cower
Beneath a passion of more power."
He left the room, his bondman called,
Who, at his visage shrank appalled ;
"Slave, to my dungeon cell convey
The Jewess saved the other day,
Disrobe her of her garb and clothe
Her in such dress as Christains loathe.
Guard well thy captive—with thy head
If she escape it will be paid."
Thus saying, waiting no reply,
    He entered in his room of state
    To seal judicially his hate,
And sign the writ that Ruth should die.

Yet on his haggard brow, the gloom
Might seem the shadow cast of doom,
That fall on such beyond the tomb.
While in this life his vengeful brain
And heart nigh bursting in its pain
Distinguish him another Cain.

XVIII.

The hours creep slowly on toward night,
The lessening sun retires from sight,
Yet, ere the stars that nightly shine
To mark the gaudy day's decline,
Have wheeled their glittering ranks in line,
The tidings wide have spread, and seem
Of speech the sole absorbing theme,
And wake such interest even pride
Ancestral, ceases to divide,
And Gentiles freely with the Jew
Untiringly the theme renew.
The victim's beauty and the doom
So awful in that beauty's bloom :

And vague insinuations thrown,
Her crime was not her faith alone,
And all the air of mystery
Of what her unknown rank might be,
During the three days given of grace,
Conjecture strives in vain to trace—
And adds more interest to the case.

XIX.

And she, the victim of his hate,
How doth she bear her altered state?
Hath dungeon fare and fear repressed
The constant courage of her breast?
The difference from her glittering room
    With all that luxury could provide
Of that damp dungeon's rayless gloom,
    Hath this, too, crushed her spirit's pride?
Nay, faith, to her unshaken breast
Hath given more than earthly rest,
As trusting Him whose presence near
Can make a prison shine with cheer,

She leans upon His faithfulness
To hold her with almighty grace,
Assured a brighter crown to wear
With Him for whom she suffers here.
She hears Him bid her troubling cease,
And feels her heart filled with His peace ;
And twice, for now two days hath flown
Since she was in the dungeon thrown,
She hath lain down to slumbers deep
As peaceful as an infant's sleep.

XX

Not so to her destroyer passed
The hours since he beheld her last.
Before his sleep-deserted eyes
In constant view her features rise ;
His mansion turned to solitude,
Where he forbade in his wild mood
Aught but his servants to intrude,
Who shudder as they pass him by,
At that mad glance and bloodshot eye.

Or by the half-closed doorway crouch
To proffer food he scarce will touch.
For there for hours he sits alone
And motionless and heeding none,
There, in that room, where oft he came
To see her whom they dare not name.
That room was hers, and is the same
As when she left it—naught is changed,
Not even a curtain disarranged.
It seems to soothe his frenzy there
To sit him down upon her chair,
   And bend his head upon his hands
   And think—but who e'er understands
The frenzied thoughts of that despair,
Which, when Remorse the spirit rends
'Twixt pride that neither sleeps nor bends,
And Conscience's reproving tone
Feels Reason totter on her throne !

XXI.

But oft he startles from the chair

With eyes that like a madman's glare,
And flees from room to gilded room,
As if he fled Orestes' doom ;
And words of more than earthly fear
Fall on each frightened bondman's ear,
And tell how in his crazy mood
He deems that fire consumes his blood,
And all apart from mortal life
His spirit writhes in deathless strife :
And round him, as within him, plays
The tortures of that endless blaze
Which is reserved unquenchable,
For those whose black lives merit hell.
Or, perhaps, recurring to its cause,
The vision that his frenzy draws
Pictures a maiden, young and fair,
Whose eyes implore his soul to spare.
   And on her naked limbs are stains
   That show the bruise of galling chains
Upon their gleaming whiteness there ;

And near her, in the act to spring,
He sees a lion balancing
That springs, but missing her, has pressed
Its shaggy form against his breast;
He feels the sharp remorseless teeth
Crush through him as he lies beneath.
So vivid is his fancy's sight
Exhausted nature faints outright;
But when revived his mind grows clear,
He curses at his frenzied fear,
And hastens to his room to hide
The shame of his unhumbled pride.

XXII.

It was the second night that fell
Since Ruth was pent in dungeon cell;
The stars were marshalled in the sky,
The moon was bright, half heaven high,
The wind had died, so calm, so still,
Not even an echo left the hill.
The Governor in his favorite room

Had seen the early shadows gloom,
And on that cloudless heaven and clear,
Had watched the glittering stars appear
As if (as ancient sybils say
There were in their prophetic ray
The destinies of men indeed)
He strove his future there to read.
Oh, long he looked along that scene,
    And seemed to feel his fevered breast
    Soothed into something like to rest ;
Beneath those rays so calm yet keen.
And long, perchance, he still had gazed,
Save as a casual eye he raised
Unto a star that shone so bright
Upon the dark blue plain of night,
He chose it for his future's flight;
When down through those still depths of air
    It fell, a luminous trail of light
    That faded into utter night.
It chilled him with a worse despair.

"The stars," he murmured, "in the sky,
Betoken curses from on high."
Nor could he wish to look again
Upon that brilliant, starry plain,
But turned, so slight a thing can change,
His heart on maddening thoughts to range.

XXIII.

Long hours that room he paces 'round
And by his footfalls' echoed sound,
Awakes the slaves who hear with dread
That hurried, tireless, ceaseless tread,
When lo! a shriek their ears appall—
A wild despairing shriek—a fall,
And then a gurgling cry of pain,
And silence ominous again :
They list a moment still to hear
That footfall echo to the ear ;
Then rush with bated breath dismayed,
And lighted tapers, to his aid,
Although their heavy hearts forbode

Their help could bring their lord no good.

XXIV.

How dread the scene that meets their sight
By the frail taper's flickering light.
There, scarcely dead, their master laid,
His body pierced through by his blade;
In his wild frenzy thus their lord
Had flung himself upon his sword.
A pool of blood drips in their view,
The floor absorbs the sanguine hue,
His body warm—his arms still shake
At the half-timid touch they make;
His eyes roll once at that mild touch,
Then close forever in reproach.
They bear him softly to the bed,
But ere they lay him he is dead.
The needless leech they send for still
Confirms the fear he has no skill;
Too sure the aim of his despair,
To leave a hope of saving there.

XXV.

To Ruth, although the deed fulfilled
The prophecy she feared, not willed,
The end so swiftly came—the blow
Subdued her heart and chilled her brow,
And fast and sympathizing fell
The first tears shed within her cell,
And more regret her lips express
Than ever for her own distress.
The jailer views, amazed, the scene
Of her, who, until now had been
In that dark cell as calm as though
She had no sense nor fear of woe,
Weep feelingly for him whose hate
Had doomed her to that awful fate.
But little could he know, and live
　'Mid scenes of battle and of strife,
　With stern revenge and rancor rife,
How much a woman can forgive.

XXVI.

It is not Battle's fiery mood
That shows the noblest fortitude.
Nor he, who dies as Brutus died
The suicide of his own pride,
Who flees from life, nor dares to meet
The scoff, the humbling of defeat,
Of Circumstance the helpless slave,
Can call his temper truly brave;
Nor he, whom pains nor dangers great
Deter not his determined hate,
Though thwarted oft, intent to range
Until it dies or wreaks revenge,
Can pluck from Truth the estimate
Of soul heroic, grand or great.
But those who could, like Ruth, thus brave
The criminal cell—the martyr's grave,
Nor yield unto the tyrant's might
Their simple loyalty to right,
And the oppressor stricken low.

Forgive his wrong and mourn his woe,
Display a heroism as high
   Above mere ignorance of fear,
As noonday sun and arching sky
   Are high o'er earth and objects here.

XXVII.

It does not to her thought occur
Th' effect his death may have on her,
How the lone hope her bosom pent,
That at the last he might relent,
With love triumphing over hate
And snatch her from that awful fate,
Was finally forever gone.
It comes though with the morrow's sun
That rising, ushers into birth
The last day she will spend on earth.
It comes but not disturbs the mind,
That fixed on heaven is resigned;
For with that vividness of faith
With which new converts spurn at death,

And long to walk in calm delight
Those scenes where Faith is changed to sight,
She feels in her impatient breast,
A yearning to embrace the test,
And win what gleams before her eyes,
The choicest hope—a martyr's prize—
Where seems a rapture in the pain,
To those who such reward obtain.
She does not boast the pangs to feel,
And her belief in blood to seal,
Without a shudder or a groan
From lacerated flesh and bone.
But as her memory pondered o'er
That host who greater sufferings bore,
Since Stephen testifying stood
And sealed his witness in his blood,
And knew how strength direct from heaven
Unto its bleeding saints was given,
She felt assured who was her trust
Would show His strength thro' her weak dust.

And prove the apostle's words ere long :
"When I am weak then I am strong."

.   XXVIII.

And yet she was a woman too,
To all her sex's instincts true—
A saint, who though of spiritual mood,
Yet had not lost her human blood—
A woman with such lovely face,
    Such grace her every motion in,
That not to praise were want of grace,
    And not to love were almost sin ;
A beauty who at times appears
Now wreathed in smiles, now bathed in tears,
Who would delight in love's young bliss—
To give and to receive a kiss ;
A woman with a woman's breast
To love, be praised, and be caressed ;
And not too much an anchorite,
Her social tastes and charms to blight,
But who could cheer a husband's life

With the devotion of a wife;
Could rouse his hopes, could soothe his fears
With every fondness that endears,
And yet with faults and human ill,
That prove her more a woman still.

XXIX.

The sun awakes—how callous still,
All nature seems to human ill,
And pitiless, on land or main,
With glory veils or mocks man's pain.
Who ever knew the sky less blue,
  The morning sun less warm or bright,
Although some sufferer lingering through
  The cooler hours of grateful night,
But feels his awful pains renew,
  And only sees to curse the light.
The battle-fields with blood bedewed,
A populous town made solitude.
Old Nature sends her thoughtless rain,
Th' unconscious flowers there spring again,

And though an empire there entombs,
She still as sweetly sings and blooms.

XXX.

Such morning dawned on Ruth's dread day,
And mocked her with its brightest ray.
The early matin lay she heard
Of many an unimprisoned bird,
Which rose above her dungeon dun,
With gladsome notes to greet the sun;
The free winds through the prison waft
The odors of the flowers they quaffed;
She heard the rustling of the trees
Swayed into motion by the breeze,
And watched the sunlight as it fell
Through the slant windows of her cell,
Until the jailer brought her food,
And thus disturbed her solitude.

XXXI.

The theater that Herod built,
    Still in its pride of beauty stood;

Its shafts elaborately hewed
From costliest white marble, filled
With hatred old Jerusalem
Whose bigotry abhorred that gem,
And scorned the efforts of his reign
To reconcile them to their pain,
And hide the subjugating chain
The tyrant forged around their rights,
By splendid domes and pleasure sites.
In vain he sought to win their hearts:
They hated him and scoffed his arts,
Yet had they known the time would come
That there would be the martyrdom
Of an apostate from their creed,
They had forgiven him the deed
In rearing close their temple by
That pile they deemed profanely nigh.

XXXII.

But never since it had been built,
Had such a gathering in it filled,

As at th' appointed time had come
To witness Ruth's harsh martyrdom;
For free to all to celebrate
His advent to his new estate,
The Governor's successor had
Unto the scene his subjects bade,
With promised drama, but the crowd
With curbed restraint, or whispers loud,
Await the final scene—in them
The music soft, the sparkling gem,
Or play-queen's mimic diadem,
Or nimble dancer ne'er at rest
Awake but little interest.
But tier o'er tier—a countless throng,
The arch and galleries among,
Await with deep impatience there
To see Ruth's advent and despair;
And even woman's gentler soul
Is barred to mercy's mild control,
And views without solicitude

The scene that sheds a sister's blood;
While on a seat apart and high,
The Governor looks with stoic eye.

XXXIII.

The longed for scene arrives—of all
The one which holds their hearts in thrall.
'Tis strange that morbid, mad delight
With which the soul can crave such sight,
That fester in the human breast,
Extreme in some, in most repressed:
And yet in all to some degree,
And fired to flame so easily,
That even the mildest, gentlest mood
Feels the contagion stir its blood
Amid a morbid multitude;
That passion, like the tiger thirst,
When once in human gore immersed,
That, satiate of former food,
Will taste no flesh but human blood.
Attest it such a scene as this,

Where beauty joins its winesses
And even in modern times again
The cruel sport of sunny Spain,
Still shows that temper fanned to flame
Without the blush of natural shame,
Where even the gentlest natures see,
With wild delight, the agony
Burning in every bleeding vein
Of helpless creatures crazed with pain.

XXXIV.

The motley crowd grew hushed as death,
And Expectation held its breath,
As, with a mighty roar, each beast
In the arena was released.
But first, the crier did advise
The crime for which the victim dies.
Such sins he charged the Christain name
As roused the mob to wilder flame,
And crushed each struggling feeling low
That pleaded pity on her woe.

The jailer led Ruth gently there,
  As if he were compassionate
  And mourned for her terrific fate,
  And scorned the multitude's wild hate
That could destroy a thing so fair;
And stood upon the parapet
  That guarded from the dangerous place,
  Where the gaunt beasts crouch low, 'or
  Each other round the enclosed space, [chase
And waited—for no signal yet,
The Governor's motionless hands display.
That he shall cast the beasts their prey.

XXXV.

A murmur 'scaped the multitude,
As there before them all she stood,
Of admiration—surely ne'er
Had e'er they seen a face more fair.
The youthful bloom was scarcely pale
Upon a cheek that told no tale
Of terror—each large lustrous eye

Had never beamed more bright and dry ;
No fear shook her undaunted breast,
But calm with peace and self-possessed,
She turned upon the populace
The sunshine of her holy gaze,
As might some heavenly creature fair,
Who for a moment had lit there,
Glance on them consciously still safe,
Howe'er their powerless rage might chafe.
So fell her glance on them—but they
Felt no remorse or pity pray
In their wild hearts, the beasts that champed
Their hungry jaws and fought and stamped
In the arena, had more grace
Than that infuriate populace.

XXXVI.

The Governor yet delays—oh say !
Hath mercy finally gained the day
And triumphed o'er the wish to slay ?
Will he forgive the Christian creed

That is to him a crime indeed?
And dare he thwart the frenzied mood
Of that bloodthirsty multitude?
In sooth, he is far more than brave
If at this hour he dares to save.
But why the pause? while wild and loud,
The clamor rises of the crowd;
He stands as if irresolute,
Attentive to a stranger's suit,
Which must be of a grave import
At such a place t' engage his thought.
Then leaning, waves his hand, to gain
Their ear and the delay explain—
"This stranger brings unto my ear
Strange tidings of a danger near;
Which, though I deem them dubious, sooth.
An hour confirms or proves untruth.
But few weeks since I only knew
Bar-Cocab as an outcast Jew,
The leader of lawless horde

Whom pillage was the sole reward,
Until the later tidings bore
Of Jew revolt from Roman power,
With him to lead the rebel force :
And then came in successive course
The news of desperate battle fought,
His force destroyed—himself uncaught.
This stranger fled from his command,
Brings me strange tidings of his band :
How that Bar-Cocab 'scaped again
Unto the remnant of his men,
From many a distant province draws
A new support unto his cause ;
Of whom th' informer here was one,
But, for some evil to him done,
And by his chief repeated long,
Now seeks revenge for his deep wrong
And will Bar-Cocab's plans betray—
Ho ! rescue ! seize her ! traitor stay !"

XXXVII.

Too late to foil the rescue planned,
　　Unknown to Ruth—by those who fled
　　That fatal field of ruin red
To grasp from his consenting hand
The prisoner whom the jailer held;
　　Who, largely bribed and fully taught,
　　All unsuspected, as he brought
　　The victim where the lions fought,
　　Had chosen a place to stand and wait
　　The Governor's signal, near a gate;
　　The farthest from the crowd, but near,
Where mounted men outside appear,
And as the stranger's word compelled
　　The Governor his tale to hear,
And for a moment to him drew
The multitude's attention too,
Few saw the treachery consummated
　　Nor marked how, springing out the gate
　　The jailer bore a lovely weight;

And joining there the three who waited,
He mounts a steed that saddled stood,
And with them galloped unpursued,
Till, by the Governor's cry recalled,
The audience beheld, appalled
And powerless then to stop them sped,
The prey they deemed secure had fled.

XXXIII.

Within a chaos reigned, that made
For his escape a welcome aid,
As, leaping from the Governor's grasp,
The stranger did his sword unclasp
And almost gained the outer door,
So fierce and fast his way he bore,
When rose a voice the uproar o'er—
"It it is Bar-Cocab's self," it cries,
Seize him ere yonder door he tries."
Already one is dead who thought
To bar the egress that he sought,
Another feels his dangerous blade:

But all in vain—the crowd have made
Concerted onslaught where he stood,
And thrown to earth, he is subdued.

XXXIX.

Loud execrations load the air
Against the captive pinioned there,
Who bravely owned his name—nor quailed
Before the hatred that assailed ;
But cast his fearless eye along
That maddened, disappointed throng,
As if amid a feast's repose
Instead of circled round with foes,
Who even of his own nation stood
Alike athirst to shed his blood.
The hearts that yesterday had bled
To save him in the cause he led,
Are turned from him who snatch'd from death
The loathed apostate from their faith,
And deem him by that act displayed
Alike with her a renegade.

XL.

His eyes roam slowly round the place,
And glance defiance at each face,
Then fall on the arena's space ;
They rested but a moment there,
To see the lions' eyeballs glare,
Yet quicker than a flash, the thought,
The fevered multitude hath caught,
"The lions!" is the awful cry ;
Such fate await the treacherous spy :
He robbed us of our sport—'tis fair
Himself another prey prepare."
That cry that more impatiently
Rolls on, may not resisted be.
They loose his bands, but unarmed yet,
They fling him o'er the parapet ;
With one wild roar that rolls along
Like thunder echoing hills among,
The lions rush upon their prey,
And crunch   *   *   *   *   *

XLI.

But Ruth, thus saved from martyr strife
A gentler evening ends her life.
Devoted by her willing vow,
To Heaven only here below,
In fasts and prayers and choral song,
And deeds of love and vigils long,
Where poverty and dread disease,
Upon their hapless victims seize.
She makes no reference to the past,
And if her thoughts are on it cast,
Th' occasional sigh alone betrays,
The memory of other days,
And so beloved and loving all,
The shadows of the long year's fall,
While she awaits with patient faith,
The hour that crowns her even in death.

Brooklyn, N. Y., October 15, 1881.

FINIS.